FidGeT the wonder dog

Patricia Forde & Rachael Saunders

PUFFIN

For Winnie and Millie, our wonder dogs – R.S.

For Róisín and Caoimhe Tuite with love from Toto – P.F.

PUFFIN BOOKS

UK | USA | Canada | Ireland | Australia
India | New Zealand | South Africa

Puffin Books is part of the Penguin Random House group
of companies whose addresses can be found at
global.penguinrandomhouse.com.

www.penguin.co.uk
www.puffin.co.uk
www.ladybird.co.uk

 Penguin
Random House
UK

First published 2020
001

Printed in China

A CIP catalogue record for this book is
available from the British Library

ISBN: 978-0-241-37316-3

All correspondence to: Puffin Books,
One Embassy Gardens, New Union Square,
5 Nine Elms Lane, London SW8 5DA

Fidget.

That's **my** dog.

Fidget is not
a fetch and carry dog

Not a lie by the fire dog

Not a cuddle up in bed dog

Not a **fetch your slippers** dog

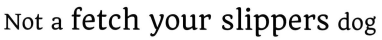

Not a **bring the paper** dog

Not a **show** dog

Not even a **pretty** dog

No.

Fidget is . . .

A jump on Granny's bed dog

A barking,
laughing,
crazy dog

A dash around the kitchen dog

A swing from the trees
like a monkey dog

A run around in circles dog

A love to ramble off dog

And once . . .

A run away
from home dog

A brave the wind
          and rain dog

A couldn't find his way dog
A sad and lonely hungry dog

A missing on a poster dog

A fill my eyes with tears dog
A smash my heart in two dog

And then he was . . .
A stowaway on a ship dog

A sail the seven seas dog

A see a mighty whale dog
A fight a gale force ten dog

A shipwrecked
and a sorry dog

A dream of the fire at home dog

A send an SOS dog

A wait

and wait

and wait dog

And then . . .

A saved . . .

. . . and brought back home dog

A run

and run

and run dog

A search and then a find dog

A meet and reunite dog
A wet my face with licks dog
A fill my arms with fur dog

A flip my heart with love dog

Yes!

Fidget is an **unusual** dog
   A **one of a kind** dog
   A **wonder** dog

   A **no one else's** dog

      A **good** dog

Fidget.

That's my dog.